STRAWS AND PRAYER-BOOKS

Dizain des Diversions

By

JAMES BRANCH CABELL

"Behold the child, by Nature's kindly law,
Pleased with a rattle, tickled with a straw. . . .
Scarfs, garters, gold, amuse his riper stage,
And beads and prayer-books are the toys of age."

The Fairmont

ROBERT M. McBRIDE & COMPANY
NEW YORK   :   :   :   :   :   :   1924

Third Edition

Published, 1924

To

BALLARD HARTWELL CABELL

*is dedicated whatever may be of worth in this
volume, or elsewhere in the Biography.*

Contents

THE AUTHOR OF JURGEN

"As to the book of the Laws composed by him, what good have they done us? And yet he ought (as Lycurgus did the Lacedæmonians, and as Solon did the Athenians, and Zaleucus the Thurians), if they were excellent, to have persuaded some to adopt them. How, then, can we consider Plato's conduct anything but ridiculous?—since he appears to have written his laws, not for men who have any real existence, but rather for a set of persons invented by him."

§ 1

"BUT this is grossly unfair!" John Charteris complained. "All these long years you have been promising to write a book about me. And now, it seems, I am to remain forever a minor character."

"Well—!" I admitted.

"And why, pray?"

"Well—!" I explained: and I went on, "I mean, of course, that is, after I had given the matter real consideration—" Then I summed it all up even more completely. "But, come now, Charteris! you, as a writer yourself, know how these submitted notions by and by come back from the cellar of what we—well, as one might say, fraudulently—term the subconscious; and come back either transmuted into something quite different or else marked Not Available for Our Present Needs."

He shook his head. "In the fidgeting face of such tergiversation I can but observe that, really, of all things! For, when one considers the persons whom you have elected to give a whole book to, civility must seek refuge in aposiopesis. Me, look you, me, you have passed over in favor of a moonstruck Kennaston and of that fat little Woods widow!"

"The Author," I pleaded, "does not customarily explain why he elects to do anything."

"None the less, I am sure I would have made a most remunerative protagonist. My inconsistencies are amusing: my whimsies, although decorous, are flavorsome: my morals are, if not exactly beyond reproach—"

"Beyond hope, anyway," I suggested.

"—And, in short, I am inclined to think that, here again, the Author does not quite understand just what he is about."

"Upon my word," said I, "you touch a truth—"

"Each has his métier," the little man admitted, modestly. "The flea leaps well, most senators carry their liquor well, whereas the clergy, one deduces from the numerousness of their children—"

§ 2

"I mean," I interrupted, "that once you talked to me all through one fine spring night. It was about Romance you talked—"

"I remember," Charteris stated, with a grin. "I

can well remember how, in that terrible dawn, after all my lovely rhetoric, you thought I had been explaining how books ought to be written."

"Well, I do not think that now. I incline, rather, to think you were talking about man's attitude toward life and the universe. I am sure, though, that in all your speaking of books you left unsettled the question you raised a moment since, as to what the Author is about? For what reason, in fine, and with what reward in view, does any author write his books?"

"I voiced for you most plainly and mellifluously the principles of his economy—"

"Yes: I remember your high observations as to Villon and Marlowe. The artist, you argued, is unwilling to be wasted; and he alone manages— sometimes—to perpetuate himself where everybody else perishes. You were quite eloquent about the artist's immortality. Only, I remember too that, toward the end, you admitted a considerable distinction. In art, you cried, it may so happen that the thing which a man makes may endure to be misunderstood and gabbled over, but it is not the man himself. We retain—I am still paying you the handsome tribute of exact quotation,—we retain the *Iliad,* but oblivion has swallowed Homer so deep that many question if he ever existed at all."

Charteris replied with something of the hasty

affability appropriate to dealings with the insane. "Now, my dear man! the whole point was that the artist strives to make something which endures—"

"I know! You explained what he attempts to do: but you did not explain why he should want to do it. You did not explain what he gets out of it,— beyond suggesting, and then retracting the suggestion, that he aspires to a sort of terrestrial immortality. No, Charteris, you explained, in fine, nearly everything connected with books except why an author writes them."

He deliberated this. He said: "Oh, but I must have made that plain. I can most vividly remember elucidating every bit of the universe, and that rather important detail could not well have been ignored."

"Ignored or not, you left it unexplained."

And promptly Charteris settled back in his chair, intent to remedy this omission.

"The author, then, very much as I did, will under provocation become magniloquent, and will say this, that and the other. But every author's real reason for writing is that, if he did not write, he would be bored to death. He writes because—"

Here I stopped him. "No, Charteris! You are too fond of juggling phrases with no better end in view than to get pleasure from your own dexterity. And I happen to be in earnest. Some twenty years and more, you conceive, I have given over, together

with health and eyesight, to the writing of the
Biography: and I am nowadays, however late in the
game, quite honestly and not unnaturally concerned
to find out why."

"So, then! at last, you sympathize with your re-
viewers!"

"It was well enough, in the beginning," I went on,
"to listen to your Economist theories: and while you
talked I could believe in them, almost. Your verbal
jugglery, I do not question, would still have that
effect. But the moment you have done talking, I
can but come back to the blunt truth, unwillingly:
the artist cannot ever by making a statue or a paint-
ing or a book—no matter how long the thing made
may last,—immortalize himself. He would come a
great deal nearer to perpetuating himself by begetting
as many children as his natural forces and the frailty
of his friends permitted—"

"Ah, the lewd Jurgen touch!" said Charteris,
regretfully.

"—And it can in no way concern the artist, either
for good or ill," I continued, "that something which
he happened to make, endures after he has perished.
No doubt, you could explain the contradiction in
your argument: you slightly married men have
learned how to explain everything. But, after all,
this is an affair in which I want my own notions,
not yours."

§ 3

"Let me have just one other book to live and talk in," Charteris said, "and I will explain the scope and aim of novel writing with such a grace and loveliness as never was! My notions have a freer wing than yours: and if you are obstinate about this, you will be encountering by and by that statement in the public prints. 'The author has here vainly endeavored to recapture the charm of his earlier *Beyond Life,* and when he speaks in his own person is by no means so amusing.' That, I forewarn you, will be the unanimous verdict."

"I do not altogether aim at being amusing. I want, rather, to wind up affairs by contriving an epilogue for the Biography."

He regarded me for some while: and I do not know how to indicate his kindly and rather commiserating pensiveness.

Presently he said: "But I forewarn you, too, that nobody is ever going to recognise the Biography as an actual fact. You may pretend to yourself, if you like, that all your writing is of this one human life reincarnated over and over again, in the flesh of Manuel's various descendants, and endlessly performing the same rôle in what is, at bottom, always the same comedy. The nearest anyone will ever come to agreement with you is to admit that you have wasted time and pains in patching up a sort of genealogy; and that your books, in fact, are—if you think it a merit,—rather monotonously the same, because you are unable to draw any figure other than yourself in a more or less transparent masquerade."

"The charge of monotony—in that word's primal sense, which you might with profit look up in the dictionary,—I acknowledge, and even glory in. For, as you say, it is perhaps the main point of the Biography that it—and human life—present for all practical purposes the same comedy over and over again with each new generation."

"Ecclesiastes, I believe, commented on the same phenomenon. Still, if you want people to read more than one of your books—"

"Not my books," I amended, "but my one book, which is the Biography, and of which my various publications are chapters."

Charteris shrugged. "My dear fellow! I, in common with the remainder of mankind, refuse to admit the possibility of anybody's writing a book in nineteen volumes. It simply is not done."

"But," he was told, with stubborn modesty, "but I have done it. Anyhow, fifteen volumes—"

"Oh, no: you have merely written fifteen books. That is a quite different affair, which anyone could manage, given pen and ink and time and a sufficient lack of consideration for one's fellows. The connection of these various books, I can assure you, is either forced or imagined: otherwise, they would be an affront to the rest of us."

"Of course," I conceded, a bit mollified, "of course, if you are putting the Biography upon a basis with Sir Thomas Browne's Relations Whose Truth We Fear—"

"I am putting, to the contrary, the author of the Biography," said Charteris, "into a phrase."

"And that phrase is—?"

Charteris grinned. "The author of *Jurgen.*"

"I begin already," I commented, "to dislike that phrase—"

"Nevertheless, you need never look to find yourself regarded as anything save the author of *Jurgen* and, just incidentally, of some other books. There, after all, my friend, the Tumble-bug has scored: and nobody, for the rest of your lifetime, will you ever hear speak of those other books except, more or less politely, to find fault with their likeness or their unlikeness to *Jurgen.* Either quality, as you perhaps have learned already, is equally to be deplored and shrugged over."

"As the subscriber to a clipping bureau," I admitted, "I have noticed the fact rather unavoidably. Any likeness to *Jurgen* is the tiresome reworking of

an exhausted vein: but any difference from *Jurgen*
proves my exhausted abilities."

Again beneath his moustache his teeth showed.
"So you remain, you see, the author of *Jurgen.*"

"Scott," I replied, "wrote *The Antiquary;* and
Thackeray wrote *Henry Esmond;* and Dickens
wrote *Our Mutual Friend:* yet people even to-day
continue to think of them as the authors, severally,
of *Ivanhoe* and *Vanity Fair* and *Pickwick Papers.*
So I suppose that nothing can be done about it."

Charteris regarded me for a lengthened while.
"I see: you have become stoically reconciled to hav-
ing posterity go on thinking of you, for century after
century, as merely the author of *Jurgen.*"

It may be that I flushed. "But, Charteris, I
never said—"

And now his shoulders went up. "My dear man!
as if you had to!"

§ 4

"Yet, in this epilogue at least," John Charteris
went on, "you may, as it happens by rare good luck,
hope to avoid the ephemeral—"

"Not utterly," I dissented. "In literary fields
there are always so many May-flies about— But
then, Charteris, I had thought to add footnotes
which would explain all such allusions—"

"As may be incomprehensible to your readers of

a few hundred years hence? I see. Such carefulness must be granted to display a kindly heart, in an illuminating blaze of self-complacency. But I was in train to suggest, my friend, that you might avoid the ephemeral by rather different methods."

"As how?" I asked.

"By listening," replied Charteris, "to me, while I discourse of eternal verities. This happens to be one of my loquacious afternoons—"

And here I raised my hand, in utterly unheeded protest.

"—For you inform me that you need for this debatable Biography," John Charteris continued, "an epilogue,—which of course ought to be spoken by the same person who afforded the prologue. Well, I shall overlook your crass misrepresentation of me in that prologue, which you so ill-advisedly called *Beyond Life*. You will remember how many 'spiritualists' turned to it with fervor, and away from it with disgust? I, none the less, forgi— .d off-hand, I would say—"

"No, Charteris! No, for I mu/ my elf contrive this epilogue—"

"But, dear man, I ha   . / ready complete, to the last paradox. It '. in my mind now, hastening to the tip of my tongue—"

"No, Charteris, I will not hear you!"

"—Art, just as Schiller long ago perceived, is an

outcome of the human impulse to play, and to avoid tedium by using up such vigor as stays unemployed by the necessities of earning a living. The artist is life's playboy. The artist, to avert the threats of boredom, rather desperately makes sport with the universe—"

"It is a universe you are quitting—"

"—For, as you of course perceive, the literary artist plays: he does nothing else, except with haste and grudgingly: and the sole end of his endeavor is to divert himself—"

But I had shaped the Parting Sign of Ageus, which is interpreted variously, but whose efficacy does not vary. . . .

§ 5

I hated thus to despatch the little fellow, after we had played together for all of twenty-two years. Besides, his going was not alone. A great many others, I suspected, departed with him: and I fancied that if, rising, I now looked out of the library window as far as the Mill Road, I might see yonder,— passing now away from me, now that our commerce was over, and travelling in motley companionship through the gray spring weather,—all the various men and women whose lives I had fashioned for me to play with in my books. Heaven only knew, if Heaven imprudently concerned itself with such matters, how many hundreds of them there must be. . . .

And now they were all gone, I turned to the task of getting down upon paper my notions as to the aims of my writing, and some explanation as to what I had been about during the years which I had given over to the compiling of the Biography of Dom Manuel's life. For the task approached completion: or, rather, the game drew toward its end; and that ending might well be the appropriate season for me to sit out, irrevocably, while the others played on.

However! once the Biography was really done, and once the volumes as yet accessible nowhere save in, as went my resources, that almost prohibitively priced Intended Edition, when these had been issued uniformly with the rest,—with the Kalki binding, and the usual number of misprints,—then I might or might not want to write something else. Or perhaps before that time came would come death. Time, either way, would settle the upshot without my aid. Meanwhile I most certainly wanted my epilogue, in the shape of a summing up which would explain, if only to me, just why I had been at pains to write this exceedingly long book,—which all other persons, whether obtusely or whether in self-protection, insisted upon regarding as *Jurgen* and several other books.

§ 6

And somehow, now that, comfortably replete with luncheon, I approach my epilogue, now it is in my mind to make verses rather than to discourse in sober and reasonable prose. But I lack any matter, too, that plainly prompts to versifying. So I somewhat vacantly consider the trees which stand about my library window. At this season they have put off their nakedness, but the green of their leaves has not yet come to its full volume. The leaves are sallow and infrequent. They dapple a luminous gray sky with much the effect of germs seen under a microscope. The grass in the long field beyond is pale and sodden: for I regard all this in a gray shining pause between the heavy spring rains. The world, in preparing to be very beautiful, is for the while disheveled looking: and it suggests to me, without any stepping stones of exact analogy, a handsome woman defamatorily clad in a shabby green dressing-gown, poised before her mirror, with her hair already partially loosened in order that she may prepare for a festival.

It is a fine festival for which the world makes ready. It is a pageant and a banqueting that will feed all the senses, and will last for months, until the white winds of November come, like gaunt janitors, to remove the furniture and decorations. Life every-

where will burgeon and exult, and bear fruit, and
wane peacefully.

I mean not only grasses and bushes and trees.
There will be a great barking of dogs, and cats also
will make the warm night vocal. And birds too will
cry out in the night, as if amazed and wistful, and
that crying will be very piercingly sweet and, for no
reason at all, pathetic. There will be lambs, and
foals, and calves, with amateurishly constructed
legs. And of course the young people— But I
wonder about those young people! There is upon
them a bland hard innocence, like the gloss of white
china. It is slippery, and it ever so lightly chills.
Yet it does seem, essentially, innocence. I recall,
with a wealth of ancient instances, that my own
generation, where it went unchaperoned, was remarkably unhampered by innocence: and I wonder
if my own generation was like this in the presence
of our elders? I do not remember; I feel that nobody could hope to remember a thing so far away:
and it is in my mind to make verses.

For I remember many other matters that have to
do with moonlight and with the touch of young flesh
and with a lost consciousness of being fearless and
eternal. Music too seems to be woven through the
background of my memories, not as a thing quite
noticed, but as not ever wholly absent. I remember,
in fine, youth: and I know that the glad magic of

youth was always a promise of whose fulfillment one lived, then, utterly assured: and I suspect that to be old means merely coming to comprehend that this promise has not been, and never will be, kept. Meanwhile I observe it is still the nature of young persons to seek out quiet places in couples, and to evince no distaste for twilight: and I surmise that even those inexplicable automobiles which stand to the side of our country roads at evening and after nightfall have at least two persons inside them. These phenomena also are a portion of the premeditated festival, of that sublimely irrational festival whose *ducdamê* (as Jaques in the play, you will remember, calls that invocation which draws fools into a circle) is still the promise which all, by and by, perceive to stay eternally unfulfilled.

Now it is in my mind to make verses about this festival, but I lack any matter, here again, that plainly prompts to versifying. We older persons must sit out, sit out forever from this especial form of recreation, while others play on. We dare at most to attend as chaperons, and with a smile to observe these junketings: for Time, that stern old Roman, states outright (in of course his native tongue), *Lusisti satis!*

I do not say that we have not equally important things to do, in our traffic with affairs of the mind: I would not assert our utter readiness, as yet, for the scrap-heap and the graven tributes of the stone-mason. I merely note that we are but, at best, the chaperons at this festival for which the April world is preparing. So we must look on benevolently, and must preserve decorum, and also must not ever concede what urge it is that prompts this festival. . . . Still, it is in my mind to make verses. . . .

§ 7

There is, though, I reflect, than this knack of sitting out at the right moment, and without sulkiness, from avocations for which the unfriendly years disqualify you, no finer, no more beneficent, and no more difficult art. To some, indeed, mere sitting out does not appear quite adequate: and there is much to be said for the contention that the key to real success in living is to die soon enough. Yet this is an un-American accomplishment: even our leaders rarely show the masterly tact of Lincoln; and the result is that most depressing list which begins with Benedict Arnold, continues with William Jennings Bryan and Aaron Burr, and so passes calamitously through the alphabet to Woodrow Wilson. There is no one of these transient inheritors of glory but has, through a mere faux-pas in longevity, impaired his chance of retaining eternal admiration and applause.

The writer, though, I think, is over-precipitate in dying at a day less than eighty. By that time he, with steadily failing faculties, will have published a deal of insufferable twaddle: but by that time, too, his name may well have become familiar to a fair number of ponderable and unliterary persons; and the excellence of his writing may be everywhere conceded as the obvious polite alternative to reading it. He has become in the cultural vista a known, not necessarily majestic, feature: he has won, in fine, to that certain undeniable assured position which no American artist anywhere can hope to secure except by prolonged survival of his talents. Longevity, indeed, is with us the one auctorial accomplishment which intelligent people can honestly esteem: we tend to share a generous national pride in all gifted persons who have painstakingly attained to our common level through the discomforts of senile decay. Time thus induces us to cherish our Longfellows and Bryants, and even to tolerate our Whitmans: it enables our Joseph Jeffersons to earn a competence upon the stage as soon as they have grown too feeble to act: and it has also persuaded us, through just this self-same sympathetic desire to gladden the last years of every striking case of mental indigence, to establish and stock our American Academy of Arts and Letters.

So I must certainly endeavor to live as long as

may prove possible. Even if I may not hope ever to be anything more than—in the phrase not utterly peculiar to John Charteris,—"the author of *Jurgen,*" there may be compensations by and by. And in fact, I turn here to thinking, with a pleasant warm thrill, about Mencken's prediction that, if I live to be eighty, I too may be elected to the American Academy. . . .

§ 8

None the less, now that I approach completion of the Biography, this may well be the time to sit out from the most high and joyous game of writing. The young are not merely at the door, they are in all the advertising columns devoted to the season's literary masterpieces, and behind most of the editorial desks. I, who was but four years ago a dangerous revolutionary upstart, begin, even among editors and publishers, to be treated with something of the gingerly respect with which one handles antique glassware or a veteran of the War Between the States. Among the really "vital" writers, still in strenuous practise of their lack of art, "the old fellow who wrote *Jurgen*" is relegated at best to the Middle or, as they playfully call it, the Muddle generation in American Letters; and I am become a relic vaguely associable with bicycles and hansom-cabs and cigar-store Indians and cast-iron deer, and other coeval items of extinct Americana.

So it may well be time, once the Biography is quite complete, for me to sit out from the game of writing, and to make sport with words no more. And *Lusisti satis* has a dreary sound, at the first hearing: yet I do not know but that it is, in reality, the aptly worded praise of attested wisdom. "You have played enough!" I shall take it to mean that I have not stinted myself at playing, that I have got out of the writing all the diversion which is allowable.

For I begin to see fine implications in John Charteris' parting statement that the artist labors primarily, even solely, to divert himself. Whatever Schiller may have said remains to me unknown: but I find this theory, of art as play, in notoriously good standing elsewhere, among many: and I find, too, by the light of experience, a great deal in this notion that the artist—or, at least, the artist who happens to be a novelist,—is life's half-frightened play-boy. . . .

I

A NOTE ON ALCOVES

"Such is the present state of the world: and the nature of the animated beings which exist upon it, is hardly in any degree less worthy of our contemplation than its other features. Yet our first attention is justly due to Man, for whose sake all other things appear to have been produced by Nature; though with so great and severe penalties for the enjoyment of her bounteous gifts, that it is far from easy to determine whether she has proved to him a kind parent or a merciless stepmother."

I.

A Note on Alcoves

§9

"THE literary artist plays: and the sole end of his endeavor is to divert himself. . . ."

Seated now at my desk, I weighed the phrase. All valid artists in letters might or might not with justice be describable as life's half-frightened playboys. I, in any event, knew that, whatever other motives might now and then have prompted me, the Biography had been written in chief for my own diversion. Whenever people had unfavorably criticised my writing—I now perceived, my first emotion had been, always, surprise at their imagining I had especially tried to give pleasure to them. I had, instead, for nearly a quarter of a century been trying with the Biography to divert myself. That might or might not be the correct principle upon which to write novels: it was most certainly a prin-

25

ciple to which I was committed in any justifying of
the form and scope of the Biography.

So I tapped out upon my typewriter, first of all,
as a self-obvious axiom, "The literary artist labors
primarily to divert himself. . . ."

§ 10

It is surprising, though, what protean gifts a
theme develops once you attempt to grapple with it.
When I was just now moved to set down on paper
my personal notions as to the form and scope and
aim of the novel, as these notions are illustrated in
the Biography, the affair seemed simple. With the
task actually begun, the typewriter-bell may hardly
tinkle thrice (for my machine is of a venerable
model) before one sees that the guide to further
composition must be that once celebrated chapter, in
I forget whose Natural History, upon The Snakes
of Iceland. It read, as you recall, "There are no
snakes in Iceland." For one perceives that the form
and scope of the novel, if not similarly non-existent,
at least stay indeterminable in lands wherein the
form and the scope of prose fiction stay limitless.

The aim, however, of the written, printed and
formally labeled novel is, I take it, to divert. Such
is (one may assume with in any event quite reputable
backing) the only aim of creative writing, and of

all the arts. But much the same sort of diversion seems to be the purpose of a staggering number of human endeavors: and it is when one considers the novels which are not formally labeled, that the theme evasively assumes all manner of shapes, and the field of prose fiction is revealed as limitless.

I do not hunt paradox. I wish in real sincerity to acknowledge that our trade of novel writing and publishing is an ineffably minor evincement of the vast and pride-evoking truth, that human beings are wiser than reason. Pure reason—I mean, as pure as human reason assays,—reveals out of hand that the main course of daily living is part boredom, part active discomfort and fret, and, for the not inconsiderable rest, a blundering adherence to some standard derived from this or that hearsay. But human beings, in this one abnegation infinitely wise, here all discard the use of their reasoning powers, which are perhaps felt here to be at least as gullible as usual: and brave men cheerily deny their immersion in the futile muddle through which they toil lip-deep. . . . Pinned to the wall, the more truthful of flesh and blood may grant that this current afternoon does, by the merest coincidence, prove answerable to some such morbid and over-colored description by people bent on being "queer": but in the admitter's mind forgetfulness is already about its charitable censorship of the events of the morning, to the intent that this amended account be placed on file with many expurgated editions of yesterday and the most brilliant romances about to-morrow. . . . For human memory and human optimism are adepts at the prevarications which everybody grasps, retails and tirelessly reiterates: these two it is who coin the fictions which every person weaves into the interminable extravaganza that he recites to himself as an accurate summing-up of his own past and future: and everywhere about this earth's revolving surface moves a circulating library of unwritten novels bound in cloth and haberdashery.

The wholesome effect of these novels is patent. It is thanks to this brace of indefatigable romancers, it is due to the lax grasp of memory and to the perennation of optimism, that nobody really needs to notice how the most of us, in unimportant fact, approach toward death through gray and monotonous corridors. Besides, one finds a number of colorful alcoves here and there, to be opened by intoxication or venery, by surrender to the invigorating lunacy of herd action, or even by mental concentration upon new dance-steps and the problems of chess and auction bridge. One blunders, indeed, into a rather handsome number of such alcoves which, when entered, temporarily shut out the rigidity and the only exit of the inescapable corridor. Life thus becomes for humankind a far different matter from

what it would seem to any merely reasonable
creature, since life's monotonous main tenor is thus
diversified by an endless series of slight distracting
interests and of small but very often positive pleas-
ures in the way of time-wasting and misdemeanor.
And in addition, as we go, all sorts of merry tales
are being interchanged, about what lies beyond the
nearing door and the undertaker's little black bag.

§ 11

These are not, though, the only anæsthetics. The
human maker of fiction furnishes yet other alcoves,
whether with beautiful or shocking ideas, with many
fancy-clutching toys that may divert the traveller's
mind from dwelling on the prevalent tedium of his
journey and the ambiguity of its end. I have not
yet, of course, come to consideration of the formally
labeled novel, for this much is true of every form
of man-made fiction, whether it be concocted by
poets or statesmen, by bishops in conclave or by
advertisers in the back of magazines. And since
memory and optimism, as has been said, are the
archetypal Homer and St. John, the supreme and
most altruistic of all deceivers, the omnipotent and
undying masters of omnipresent fictive creation,
their "methods" are in the main pursued by the great
pair's epigoni; who likewise tend to deal with the

large deeds of superhuman persons seen through
a glow of amber lucency, not wholly unakin to that
of maple syrup.

Of the romances which make for business pros-
perity and religious revivals and wars to end war
forever, here is no call to speak. Nor need I here
point out that well-nigh everyone who anywhere
writes prose to-day, whether it take form as a tax
return or a magazine story or a letter beginning "My
dear So-and-so," is consciously composing fiction:
and in the spoken prose of schoolrooms and courts
of law and social converse, I think, no candid person
will deny that expediency and invention collaborate.
It may be true that lies have short legs, but civiliza-
tion advances upon them.

§ 12

I, in any event, get daily bewilderment from considering how deep-rooted seem all life's serious and
practical endeavors in implausible fictions. The most
long-headed of us, for instance, may reasonably
confess to some faith in money and in mathematics:
these things at least are stable realities, these are the
pillars, the very Bohas and Jakin in the Temple of
Common-Sense. And yet, here also, is disclosed by
two minutes' consideration another side.

Money I regard, I hope, with all appropriate

gravity. I know that I now and then accept without derisory outcry, even thankfully, small metal disks disfigured with a remarkably unaquiline eagle and the fat-jowled head of a female criminal very neatly guillotined. Nor am I here deceived by appearances. These things suggest extremely rococo poker-chips, they look like counters to be used in playing some sort of game, for the sound reason that this is precisely what they are. And we play. We all play quite gravely, at every hour in our lives, at the game wherein these disks, which in themselves no mortal could regard with æsthetic pleasure or employ for any imaginable practical purpose, are supposed to be worth something. In time we get quite used to these horary excursions of fancy: and indeed we so enter into the spirit of the game as very often to "buy" things with a feeling that the clerk is swindling us, rather than we him.

But, as an even more remarkable fiction, I consider the new five-dollar bill which I chance this morning to possess. In itself, like the metal disks, it is worth nothing: and its glazed surface chills the thought of devoting it to the one use suggested by its general dimensions. It bears, though, I find, an engraved assurance that to the bearer of this paper the People's National Bank of Strasburg, Virginia, will pay five dollars.

Since, as it happens, the president and the cashier

of that institution have not signed in the spaces re-
served for them, the assurance comes unsupported:
for it nobody, so far as I can see, assumes any least
responsibility. Yet, in any event, if the unsponsored
statement be true, such is the sole value of this paper
rectangle: its only virtue is that in Strasburg, Virginia, you can exchange it for five dollars.

I have no intention of going to Strasburg, Virginia: I shall instead buy something with this note,
under the romantic pretence that the shopkeeper is
going to exchange it, in Strasburg, Virginia, for five
dollars. And he will part with it to somebody else
on the same imaginative terms. And that make-
believe will continue until this note is worn out.
Meanwhile this bit of paper will gravely be exchanged, in varied surroundings, for every sort of
commodity. . . . It will be transmuted into dinners,
it will tread the pavements of remote outlandish cities
in the form of a pair of shoes, and as pajamas it
will pass beyond the proper scope of my meditations.
It will flower into orchids, it will blaze as coal. Not
without ostentation will it fall into the collection
plate, nor toward Christmas flutter into the kettle of
the Salvation Army: more furtively will it, thrice-
folded, slip into the top of the feminine stocking.
Darkness will sometimes engulf it like a pocket.
Very deep will it descend, as fares the sewer rat,
into grim social underworlds; as most inferior

whiskey it will be swallowed up; and in the manner of the dead that are laid away, will it go down into the steel catacombs beneath banking houses. Thence presently it will arise. It will arise unchanged, a trifle deteriorate in crispness perhaps, yet very potent to aid in lifting mortgages, in raising children, and in elevating many households, I would like to think, in the avatar of two of my books. . . . But never on any forenoon in Strasburg, Virginia, will it be exchanged for five dollars: and the one purpose for which this paper is so precisely designed is precisely the one to which it will not ever be put.

What will in point of fact become of it, I learn after serious inquiry into this mystery—in financial circles, wherein I was humored as a harmless lunatic,—is that, when the note gets sufficiently dirty and decrepit, "some bank will turn it in, at Washington," in exchange for a fresh paper rectangle; and the senior note will then be destroyed by Treasury employees. But nobody will ever convey to Strasburg, Virginia, this representation of Benjamin Harrison looking like a dishonest Santa Claus, and of the Pilgrims putting ashore at Plymouth Rock to investigate the phenomena of a wind that blows two ways and of a tree growing from the ocean. Nobody will ever deal logically with all this intricate engraving: and if anybody ever did, he would, as the very cream of this monetary fiction, be thought "queer." At worst, his sanity would become a matter of medical investigation: at best, he would be given for this paper rectangle another banknote, and the romancing would now gild a different Carcassonne.

And similarly outrageous seem to any calm considering the fictions of mathematics. This fact, indeed, was recently pointed out to me by my small son, in whom his governess was endeavoring to implant the conviction that two and two make four. But the child stayed sceptical. He was reservedly polite about a rational "Suppose you had two apples, and I gave you two more apples, how many apples would you have then?" He conceded with readiness, not unflavored with resignation to the obtuseness of grown-up persons, that in such circumstances he would have four apples, but could not eat that many without being real sick. Yet that two and two, in consequence, make four, he excluded as a logical inference: and he depreciated that inference by stating it did not mean anything. He was, of course, quite right.

For that "two and two make four" becomes, the very instant that you play this familiar axiom the childish trick of thinking about it, at best an unprovable hypothesis. That two apples and two more apples compose four apples is, as my son admitted, plain enough. Or, you may change your unit to a penny, a match, a pencil, or to a bungalow, and still produce convincing evidence to prove your arithmetic. But the mathematician requests us to consider an abstract "two," to believe in two apples with the pomaceousness removed: his incorporal and incorporeal "two" has never existed and never can exist. His "two" is not merely a fiction, but an inconceivable fiction which the human mind can no more, really, imagine than it can his "four." You need only for one moment attempt to form some rational and clear-cut idea of this "two" to perceive that the governess in fact was (with all respect to her) talking about incredible fictions, just as my son affirmed. . . . And when the mathematician goes on from "two" and "four" into the higher branches of his romance weaving, and postulates as yet other realities his "lines" that have length but no breadth or thickness, or his "points" that have not even length, you face the choice between fleeing from his self-evident lunacy and accepting his insane but very useful fictions.

§ 13

So do we all exist as if in a warm grateful bath, submerged and soothed by fiction. In contrast to the inhabitants of the Scilly Islands, who are reputed to have lived by taking in one another's washing, so do we live by interchanging tales that will not wash.

There seems to be no bound, no frontier trading-post appointed anywhere to this barter of current fiction, not in the future nor in the years behind. . . . Men have been, almost cynically, shown with what ease the romance which we call history may be recast throughout, now that America rejoices in an amended past which has all been painstakingly rewritten with more care of the King's English, and wherein the War of the Revolution takes its proper place as the latest addition to the list of German outrages. State legislatures dispose of man's arboreal ancestry by passing a law against it: and Congress, by bestowing upon non-intoxicating beverages an illegal alcoholic content, at once repeats and repudiates the miracle of Cana. Our newspapers continue the war-time economizing of intelligence, and still serve patriotic substitutes in serials, wherein Black and Yellow and Red perils keep colorful the outlook, and fiends oppose broad-minded seraphim in every political difference. Our clergy are no less prolific in their more futuristic school of art, and on every Sabbath morning discourse engagingly of paradise and of that millennium of which the arrival is at present being furthered by the more "modern" of our prelates bringing fearlessly to bear upon the mystery of the Incarnation the intellect of a midwife. . . . The past, the present and the future are thus everywhere presented in the terms of generally diverting prose fictions: and life is rendered passable by our believing in those which are most to our especial liking.

§ 14

Man is, they say, the only animal that has reason; and so he must have also, if he is to stay sane, diversions to prevent his using it. Man, always nearing and always conscious of approaching death with its unpredictable sequel, and yet bored beyond sufferance by the routine of his daily living, must in this predicament have playthings to divert him from bringing pitiless reason to bear upon his dilemma: and he must have too the false values which he ascribes to these playthings.

The lines of Pope that I have quoted elsewhere dwell truthfully enough upon life's endless playing,—upon the playing of the child with straws and rattles, of the young man with his mistresses, of the mature with wealth and worldly honors, and of the aged with rosaries and prayer-books. But the solace, the true virtue, of these playthings arises from the fiction that the player tells to himself about them. No child plays with a straw: he brandishes a sword that has just chopped off a dragon's head. The young man, exultant, terrified, touches and uncovers, not an expanse of epidermis and small hairs and sweat glands, but the body of a goddess. The

banker is reveling in that romance about Strasburg,
Virginia: and the aged clasp not a prayer-book but
the key to eternal bliss. Everywhere, in fine, the
creating romantic who lives in every human being is
either composing or else borrowing the kind of
romance which most potently diverts him, and pre-
vents his going mad.

§ 15

Well, it is the privilege of the novelist—I mean,
at last, the novelist who is frankly listed as such in
Who's Who—to aid according to his abilities in
this old world-wide effort, so to delude mankind that
nobody from birth to death need ever really bother
about his, upon the whole, unpromising situation in
the flesh. It is the privilege of the novelist who
happens also to be an artist, to blaze a trail upon
which his readers may follow, and be delighted by
the by-products of his hedonism. For it is his
higher privilege to divert his own thoughts from
unprofitable and rational worrying; and to lead such
as may choose to follow him in one more desperate
sortie from that ordered living and from the selves
of which all men are tired.

So I suspect there must always be, to the last digit,
precisely as many "methods" as there are novelists.
For the endeavor of the novelist, even by the lowest